About the author

Ann Jungman is the author of over one hundred books for children, specialising in mythical monsters being tamed by the modern world.

Ann was born in London and still lives there, apart from two months spent annually in Australia. Her most recent titles are ***The Prince Who Thought He was a Rooster and Other Jewish Stories*** (Frances Lincoln), and ***Betrayal!*** (Barrington Stoke) and ***The Footballing Frog*** (Harper Collins).

Ann is also the managing director of Barn Owl Books.

Other books by Ann Jungman

BROOMSTICK SERVICES
BROOMSTICK REMOVALS
BROOMSTICK RESCUES
BROOMSTICK BABY
SEPTIMOUSE SUPERMOUSE
SEPTIMOUSE BIG CHEESE
SEPTIMOUSE AND THE CHEESE PARTY
THERE'S A TROLL AT THE BOTTOM OF MY GARDEN
THERE'S A TROLL AT THE BOTTOM OF MY STREET
THERE'S A TROLL AT THE TOP OF MY TIP
Published by Catnip

VLAD THE DRAC
VLAD THE DRAC RETURNS
VLAD THE DRAC SUPERSTAR
VLAD THE DRAC VAMPIRE
VLAD THE DRAC DOWN UNDER
BOLD BAD BEN THE BEASTLY BANDIT
Published by Barn Owl Books

THE PRINCE WHO THOUGHT
HE WAS A ROOSTER
AND OTHER JEWISH TALES
Published by Frances Lincoln

Ann Jungman

Frank N Stein

and the

GREAT GREEN GREEDY GARBAGE

MONSTER

Illustrated by Jan Smith

BARN OWL BOOKS

157 Fortis Green Road, London, N10 3LX

First published by Orchard Books, 1996 as *The Monster Idea*

This edition published by Barn Owl Books, 2008
157 Fortis Green Road, London, N10 3LX

Distributed by Frances Lincoln,
4 Torriano Mews, Torriano Avenue, London, NW5 2RZ

ISBN 978 190301572 8

Designed and typeset by Skandesign Limited
Produced in Poland by Polskabook

www.barnowlbooks.com

CONTENTS

A Monster Idea

'Mark?'

'Yes, Miss.'

'Gary?'

'He's ill, Miss.'

'Frank?'

'Yes, Miss.'

'Jason?'

'Yes, Miss.'

'Good, everyone here except Gary. Now let's see, who's sitting up very straight? Mark what a lovely straight back, can you take the register to the office.'

Mark came back into the room giggling to himself and whispered something to Jason, as he sat down. They both stared hard at Frank and tried not to laugh.

At break Frank was kicking a football around on his own and wondering how long it would take to make friends at this new school, when Mark came up to him and shouted.

'Your name's Frank N. Stein. I saw it in the register. You're a monster, Frankenstein.'

A group of laughing boys gathered round Frank.

'So, what does the "N" stand for Frankenstein?'

'Norman,' sighed Frank. 'After my grandad.'

For about the five hundredth time in his life Frank wished his parents had thought before they chose his names. Frank *or* Norman, but not both together. Even Norman Frank would have been all right, but this way it was nothing but trouble.

'You've got it all wrong,' Frank explained wearily. 'Frankenstein was a scientist who made the monster, Dr. Victor Frankenstein. The monster didn't have a name.'

'Oh,' said Achmed looking puzzled. 'I always thought the monster was called Frankenstein.'

'So did I,' insisted Mark. 'You're pulling our leg, Frankenstein.'

'I am not,' said Frank indignantly. 'If you look at the book you'll see.'

There was a moments silence as the group took this in.

'I've got a great idea, why don't we help Frankenstein build a monster,' suggested Achmed who was always having good ideas.

'Great idea!' shouted Chris, 'Let's do that, let's build a mega monster.'

Achmed and Chris's excitement was catching. Soon all five boys were fired with enthusiasm for building the best and biggest monster ever. Frank even began to think his name wasn't so bad after all. It had certainly helped to make him friends at his new school.

And it would be fun building a monster.

'The problem,' said Achmed, 'is where to build it. We can't build it at school. This has to be top secret.'

'No, of course not here,' snapped Mark, who was bossy and always liked to be in charge, and was a bit annoyed that the monster hadn't been his idea. 'After school somewhere.'

'Could I say something please,' said Jason. Everyone looked at him. Jason rarely said anything.

'We could meet in my dad's garage and make our monster there.' volunteered Jason. 'My dad is away working for two weeks and he's taken the car. My mum comes home quite late from work, she wouldn't notice what we were up to.'

'Sounds great,' said Mark, taking charge. 'Can everyone come tonight?'

They all nodded.

'Right then. Everyone has to bring something to start the monster going. See you at Jason's garage about four o'clock.'

That afternoon Frank turned up with the battered door of an ancient car, Achmed brought a cracked vase, Chris brought some material his mum had thrown away and Mark arrived triumphantly with a battered suitcase full of newspapers. Jason had found an old tyre in his dad's garage. The five boys surveyed their loot.

'Right,' said Achmed, looking at Mark. 'Professor Frankenstein should be in charge. Come on, Professor, you tell us how to build this monster.'

For days the boys turned up at the garage with a vast variety of bits and pieces. The garage looked like a bomb had hit it. Glue, sticky tape, cardboard boxes, paper, paints, scissors and the contents of Jason's dad's tool box littered the floor. Mark had even found some chicken wire one day, which made an excellent framework for the body. The boys couldn't wait to finish school each day so they could get on with their building

plans. Slowly Frank's initial drawing of a monster began to materialize until it looked like a real monster.

The huge creation lay on the floor of the garage sitting up against the back wall. It was as long as the garage and nearly as high. Frank had to stand on a ladder with two orange light bulbs for eyes and ears made out of egg box cartons.

The boys stood back and admired their work. It had been worth all the days of hard work. They had built the best mega monster ever.

'He's fantastic,' breathed Frank.

The monster was almost life-like.

'*Could* you bring it alive, Frankenstein?' asked Achmed.

'Course not,' sniffed Frank. 'We'd need a proper laboratory with all kinds of machines and equipment and electrodes and things. Even then, in the book it only happens because he uses the power of lightning to give the monster life.'

At that moment there was a clap of thunder and the boys heard rain beating down on the roof.

'We'd better not go home till the rain stops,' said Mark. 'Let's play a game or something to make the time go quicker.'

'Actually, it's a bit scary in here with the monster,' commented Chris.

'Don't be ridiculous,' replied Frank. 'It's just made out of all the bits and pieces we brought here – you couldn't be frightened of that.'

'Well, let's hope there isn't any lightning,' said Jason a bit nervously. 'Let's hope the rain stops soon.'

Just then a flash of lightning sped past the tiny window in the garage and seemed to streak into the building.

'Of course there's lightning,' said Frank. 'There's always lightning when there's thunder.'

'Quite right,' came a strange voice 'Always lightning with thunder. Now, where am I?'

Horrified, the boys looked at the monster. It was very slowly sitting up and looking round. None of them could believe their ears or their eyes. The boys just huddled in a corner of the garage and stared.

Alive!

'Well,' boomed the monster. 'Where am I?'

'Um, er,' stammered Frank N. Stein. 'You are in a garage in England.'

'Oh,' said the monster. 'England. Well it's a good thing that I speak English then. Now I'm hungry. How about getting me a little something for my tea?'

The boys continued to huddle in the corner and shook with fear.

'What kind of something?' whispered Frank.

'I'm not fussy,' said the monster. 'I'll eat almost anything.'

No one moved. They were frozen to the spot.

'Well, if you're not going to bring me anything,' said the monster, 'I'll go and search for food myself.'

'No!' shouted Frank N. Stein quickly. 'Here try this!' and he picked up some wood shavings off the floor.

The monster munched away and then smiled. 'That was quite nice,' he said, 'Not a bad little snack at all.'

The five boys stared at him with fascination.

'You can eat anything in here except us,' Frank told him. 'Eating people is strictly forbidden.'

'Don't talk so daft,' grumbled the monster. 'Why should I want to eat people, they don't look tasty at all.'

The boys breathed a sigh of relief. Achmed picked up some broken china left over from making the monster.

'Here try this.'

The monster ate it and licked his lips.

'Delicious,' he declared. 'I wouldn't mind a bit more of that.'

Soon the monster had eaten everything in the garage, including Jason's dad's tools.

'I feel quite full up now,' he assured the boys. 'Think I'll have a little sleep.'

For a moment the boys were too stunned to say anything. It was incredible. The monster they had built out of cardboard boxes and chicken wire had come alive.

'We weren't dreaming were we?' Frank asked excitedly. 'He did really move and talk, didn't he?'

There was no doubt about it. The monster was now snoring.

Jason was nearly in tears. 'I suppose we'll have to tell our parents,' he cried. 'My dad will go nutty.'

'We don't have to tell anyone for a few days,' said Frank. 'We made him, we've got to keep him and look after him, at least for a little bit. He'll be our secret.'

'But then what, Frank? We can't just leave him here,' said Achmed.

Jason agreed. if they let the monster go his mum and dad need never know what happened. Although how he was going to explain the mess in the garage didn't bear thinking about.

It was obvious that no one was going to come up with an idea that night. The events of the last hour were too amazing for anyone to think properly. Instead, they agreed to talk again in the morning.

In the meantime, the boys needed to make sure the monster didn't get hungry. He seemed to like rubbish so the boys scoured the neighbourhood for dustbins and lined up thirty two black bags for the monster to eat.

Frank gently shook the monster.

'Monster, monster, wake up a minute.'

The monster rolled over and looked at Frank.

'We've got to go now. We're all coming back to see you tomorrow and bring you more food. We've left something really delicious for you over there, in case you get hungry.'

'Smells good,' commented the monster.

'You're looking after me really well. You're my boy Frank. Take care and I'll see you tomorrow.'

None of the boys slept very well that night.

At school the next day they went into a corner of the playground to continue their discussions about what to do next.

'Let's keep him a secret for ever,' said Achmed. 'We could be the only people in the world to have a real live monster.'

'I think we should confess. Tell our parents or got to the police,' sighed Jason. 'Whatever we do we're going to be in big trouble, maybe we should just get it over and done with. My dad is coming home in two day's time.'

'After school we'd better talk to the monster and see what he wants,' said Frank. 'Maybe he will have an idea. Everyone bring a dustbin with them.'

That evening they sat round the monster while he ate his way through all the rubbish they had brought him. The garage was beginning to smell terrible.

'You can't stay here for ever,' Frank told him gently. 'What do you want to do with yourself?'

'I want to stay with you, Frank,' the monster told him. 'You're my boy Frank. That's all I want, and a lot of food.'

'You really enjoy eating rubbish?'

'Well, I like eating this. If this is rubbish, then yes, I enjoy eating it.'

'I've got a brilliant idea,' shrieked Achmed. 'We could set up a Monster Show and charge all our friends to come and see him. We'd be rich!'

'Yeah,' agreed Chris. 'We made him, why shouldn't we make money out of him?'

'What's money?' boomed the monster, between mouthfuls.

'This,' said Mark pulling a handful of coins out of his pocket.

The monster looked at it, sniffed it and then swallowed the lot.

'Delicious,' he pronounced. 'You get more of that and I'll eat it.'

'I don't think that idea will work somehow, Achmed,' laughed Frank. 'You'd lose more money than you earned.'

The next day at school, Jason reminded them they only had one day left before his father came back.

'We'll have to move him tonight. I've thought about it, it's the weekend, we could put him in the school shed and that would give us a few extra days.'

As soon as school finished they rushed over to the garage, opened the garage door, and peeped out.

'All safe,' whispered Jason.

But just then a car swept down the road and into the drive.

'Oh no! Oh my goodness! It's my dad,' groaned Jason. 'He's come home early. We're for it now.'

'Hello Jason, Hello boys,' called Jason's dad. 'Open the garage doors properly please.'

'We can't dad,' Jason mumbled. 'We've got a monster in there.'

'Bit old for that kind of joke aren't you?' said his father getting out of the car. 'Well, I can see I shall have to open the doors myself.'

He flung the door open and saw the monster standing there looking confused.

'What is going on around here?' yelled Jason's dad. 'What is that thing?'

'That thing is my monster,' Frank told him. 'My name is Frank N. Stein and we built the monster for fun and he came alive in a thunder storm.'

'Now you stop this nonsense young man. I want the truth.'

'It is true, Dad,' cried Jason. 'But he's a harmless monster. All he does is eat rubbish. Ask him.'

'Now listen you lot. I've had enough of this. I have had a very busy couple of weeks, I have driven a very long way, and I've been looking forward to getting home.

So if this rubbish is not out of my garage in the next half an hour there will be real trouble.'

'Yes, Dad. Sorry Dad. we just didn't expect it to come alive,' he mumbled looking at his feet.

'Don't be hard on the lad,' boomed the monster. 'He didn't mean any harm.'

Jason's dad stepped back in amazement, 'He can talk!'

'Course I can talk,' grumbled the monster. 'What do you think I am, stupid or something? Now where's my tea? Ooo, that looks nice,' and to everyone's horror he began to eat Jason's dad's car.

'What's he doing!' yelled Jason's dad going white with anger, 'Stop him! Right that's it! Stay where you are while I go and phone the police. This is definitely an emergency!'

Kidnapped?

'They're gong to hurt my monster,' said Frank, on the verge of tears. 'And I'm not having it. I'm going to take him away to somewhere safe.'

'But Frank, where will you take him?' asked Achmed. 'You're new here, you don't know your way around.'

'I'm not sure. Somewhere where there will be plenty for him to eat. Now, we'll go out the back way. You keep the people occupied as long as you can. I want to get my monster as far away as possible.'

'Are we going somewhere, Frank?' asked the monster. 'I don't want to go away. I like it here.'

'Well, you can't stay. People will be terrified of you and there's no knowing what they will do to you.'

'Scared of me!' laughed the monster. 'I wouldn't hurt a fly.'

'Well they won't believe it,' Frank told him desperately. 'Now, come on Monster. Pick me up and then we must move off as fast as possible.'

'If you say so Frank,' grinned the monster and, picking Frank up, he pushed down the back wall of the garage and started to walk through the back gardens of the adjoining houses. The boys waved goodbye.

'Good luck,' they called.

Just then they heard the wail of a police siren. A police car screeched to a halt outside Jason's house. Jason's father came out of the house to meet it.

'Was it you who called us, Sir?' asked the policeman. 'With some nonsense about a monster nine feet tall who ate your car?'

'I know it sounds absurd,' said Jason's dad mopping his brow. 'But I'm not crazy, really I'm not. My son here and his friends made a monster and, well, he'll tell you the rest.'

'Right,' said the policeman. 'You tell me, sonny, and you'd better make it good. We police officers are busy people and we don't like having our time wasted.'

Jason looked anxiously at his friends. Mark and Achmed nodded to him frantically. So Jason turned to the policeman and explained about the monster and how he came into being and ended:

'So, you see, Sir, it was all caused by him being called Frank N. Stein. But you don't have to worry because the monster is quite harmless.'

'Harmless,' shouted Jason's dad. 'Harmless! Funny idea of harmless you boys have. he ate my car! That car cost a fortune. Just you wait till you have to pay for your own things, you'll sing to a different tune then.'

The policeman made a note in his book. 'The accused ate one pale blue saloon car.'

'What we mean is, he doesn't harm people. All he wants to do is eat rubbish,' Mark told them.

'Yes, well that's all well and good but we

can't take any risks. Think I'd better call in some back-up support.' And so saying the policeman got on his radio and did a lot of earnest talking. It seemed ages before he finally put the radio down. Then things started to happen very fast. Suddenly there were police cars blocking both exits to the street, the whirring of helicopters above, and fire engines came swinging into the street from both ends.

The Police Inspector came up to the group and explained that the first plan of action was to get the monster and Frank out of the garage. He got out a loud hailer.

'You in there, come out with your hands up and don't try any nonsense.'

Nothing happened.

Mark whispered to Jason 'I hope they've managed to get a fair distance by now.'

'Sir,' called Achmed. 'They may be

scared. Shall I go into the garage and try to persuade them to come out?'

'We'll give you two minutes and then if you don't come out, we'll have to go in.'

'I'll tell them, Sir,' said Achmed catching the eyes of the other boys.

After two minutes Achmed came out.

'No luck,' he said. 'They refuse to come.'

'Prepare to storm the garage,' commanded the Police Inspector. At a signal from the Inspector, the police officers rushed towards the garage, flung open the door, and saw that it was empty and the back wall broken.

'We're getting reports over the radio that the monster was seen carrying the boy off,' cried a police officer, getting out of a car. 'They were heading towards the hills.'

'That poor boy,' groaned Jason's father. 'He didn't realise what he was doing when he created that creature. I'd better ring his parents. Stein did you say? Oh dear, oh dear! Kidnapped by a monster, I don't know how they'll cope with the news.'

'Have you boys any idea where they might have gone?' demanded a policeman. 'You realise your friend is in great danger.'

'No, he's not,' exclaimed Achmed. 'The monster is very gentle. Frank is quite safe.'

'That's enough from you, young man,' said the Police Inspector. 'You tricked us pretending to talk them into coming out when you knew they were well away. Now, I want you boys to get off home. Let us know if you hear anything, and please, please don't go making any more monsters.'

As they went Achmed whispered to Chris,

'I bet I know where they've gone. The rubbish dump! It's the obvious place! Grab what food you can and a blanket or whatever might be useful and meet me up there. Tell Mark and Jason but don't let anyone else hear you.'

Meanwhile, Frank and the monster were sitting in the town rubbish dump. The monster was eating away.

'Nice place this Frank. Thanks for bringing me here.'

'Glad you like it,' muttered Frank who was beginning to feel cold and hungry and a bit afraid. Also the smell of the rubbish was overpowering.

Just as Frank was praying that they wouldn't have to spend long there, he looked up and saw Mark coming towards them. Breathing a sigh of relief Frank waved, the monster grinned and waved too. Mark scrambled down and handed Frank a hamburger and a can of cola. Frank gulped them down.

'What do you reckon now, Frank?' asked Mark.

'It's only a matter of time before they find us,' Frank replied grimly. 'I just wish I could think of a way to convince them that our monster is really nice and friendly.'

They sat for a while and then Mark yelled, 'I've got it! Let's get all the kids to come here to the rubbish dump and defend the monster. If the police and our parents and everyone see that we're safe with him, maybe they will be kinder to him.'

'Great idea!' said Frank. 'On your bike, Mark. Tell as many kids as possible.'

Mark rushed home and grabbed his tea before going off to Achmed's house.

The two boys rang all their friends and told them the plan.

'Pass it on,' they cried. 'We want as many kids there as possible. We need everyone's help to save the monster.'

Over the next hour dozens of children turned up at the rubbish dump.

'We told our parents we were going to bed early because we were scared of the monster,' they told Frank. 'No one knows we're here. They'd all have a fit.'

'Daft,' said the monster. 'Daft, that's what they are.' And he sat with children swarming over him laughing and playing.

As it got dark Jason turned up in his pyjamas. 'I had a terrible time getting away. I climbed out of the window. Frank, you're on the news. It's making headlines. They're saying the monster kidnapped you. Police are combing the whole area. It can't be long before they get here.'

Jason was right. Within five minutes the dump was surrounded by cars. The police loud hailer announced: 'Frank N. Stein are you there. Are you all right?'

'Yes, of course I'm here and of course I'm all right.'

'Brave boy, No joke being kidnapped. Hang on and we'll have you out in no time.'

'Frank, darling,' came his mother's voice over the loud hailer, 'We've been so worried. I'm so sorry we called you Norman as your second name. Now co-operate with the police and tell them the best way to get you out alive.'

'No problem, Mum,' Frank yelled back, 'I can come out any time I like. But there are about fifty of us children here. And we won't come out until you promise to listen to us.'

'*Fifty* children!' shouted the Police Inspector. 'Turn those lights on to the dump, I want to see for myself.'

The car lights shone down on the dump. There sat the monster surrounded by defiant children.

'It's true,' groaned the policeman. 'All right Frank. We're listening.'

'We'll come out if you give the monster a chance. All he wants to do is eat rubbish. None

of us children are frightened of him, we saw that he was nice and kind straight away. I've never met a person as nice as my monster. He's terrific.'

'I see,' said the Inspector. 'Then come on out and we guarantee that nothing bad will happen to your friend if he behaves.'

So led by Frank N. Stein holding the monster's hand all the children scrambled out of the rubbish tip. As they emerged lights flashed and news cameras rolled.

Franks' parents rushed up to him and hugged him. In front of the cameras, Frank introduced the monster to his parents.

The monster grinned and held out his hand. 'Delighted to meet the parents of my boy Frank.' he said shaking Mrs Stein's hand very hard.

The other children stood round watching. They all smelled horrible after their time in the rubbish dump. The Police Inspector held his nose.

'May I suggest that we get these children home and bathed before we go any further. Quick into the police cars, five to a car and no arguments.'

The children waved as they were driven away.

'Bye monster!' they shouted.

'Byeee,' yelled the monster back. 'Thanks for all your help. See you soon.'

'Now,' said the Police Inspector, trying to regain control of the situation, 'I'm afraid that we are going to have to take this monster to a police laboratory and do some experiments on him.'

'Must you?' groaned Frank N. Stein.

'I don't mind,' said the monster amicably. 'So long as I get some nice food and my boy Frank stays with me, I don't mind where I go.'

Steinasaurus Rex

Frank N. Stein and his monster were led to a police van. Lines of policemen stood either side of them. The monster smiled at the police and patted them on the head as they walked by. Together Frank and his creation got into a van. A policeman put handcuffs on the monster, who looked pleased and ate them in two seconds.

'Please, sir,' said Frank. 'Could my monster have some rubbish to be going on with otherwise he might start to eat the van.'

'Good thinking,' said the Police Inspector and soon some of the rubbish from the tip was in the van with Frank and the monster. As the van set off the television crews and the journalists waved.

Frank and the monster were put in the biggest room that could be found. A policeman brought them a pack of cards to help pass the time. When the monster ate them another set was brought and Frank taught the monster to play snap.

After a while a team of police scientists turned up to examine the monster.

'We would just like to carry out a number of tests,' explained the Chief Scientist. 'They won't take long and it won't hurt.'

Soon the monster was laid out on a table and a team of doctors and scientists examined him. They took his temperature and felt his

pulse, gave him injections and tested his reflexes, took a sample of the materials he was made from and put electric impulses on his head and arms and feet, and made charts. The monster smiled all the way through and did exactly as he was told. He giggled when they tickled his feet and ate the doctor's stethoscope but otherwise his behaviour was perfect. After that the scientists decided that the monster was completely harmless and the Chief Scientist went in to talk to Frank and his monster.

'We think you should have a name, monster. So what would you think of Steinasaurus Rex?'

'After my boy Frank?' grinned the monster. 'Yes. I like that.'

'Now that we know that you are not dangerous we have to decide what you are going to do, and we were wondering if you could help us with a great problem?'

'Course,' agreed Steinasaurus Rex. 'If I can.'

'Rubbish! That's the problem. Lots and lots of it. We have people to collect it but it's more difficult to get rid of it. How would you feel about going round rubbish tips and . . . um . . . eating them up?'

'Oh, yes please!' said Steinasaurus Rex, 'When can I start?'

The next Monday Steinasaurus Rex was taken to three rubbish tips and they were cleared in six hours. He couldn't have been happier.

Soon Steinasaurus Rex was travelling all over the country, eating up rubbish in England,

Scotland, Wales and Ireland. Everywhere he went, he was cheered. He became a national hero, appearing on television game shows (once he'd learnt not to eat the cameras), opening village fetes and even having a wax work made of him.

They even had to use a lot of wax because, with all the rubbish he was eating, Steinasaurus Rex was getting very big indeed!

But the bigger he got, the happier he got, and the cleaner the country got, too. Everyone agreed it had been a fortunate day when Frank N. Stein and his friends had made Steinasaurus Rex.

A Very Royal Occasion

Frank N. Stein.s most exciting day of all came when he received a letter from Buckingham Palace. It was an invitation for Frank and his parents, Jason, Achmed, Chris and Mark to take Steinasaurus Rex to a garden party.

'We'll see to it that you're fed before you go,' Frank's mum told him firmly. 'And when we get to the palace you'll have to behave.'

When the day came for them to go they all dressed up in their best clothes and Steinasaurus Rex wore a bow tie. As soon as they arrived the Queen came up to them to congratulate them on the excellent work Steinasaurus Rex was doing and she pinned a medal on the monster's chest.

'I was afraid I wouldn't get any tea here, it is very thoughtful indeed of you to provide me with such a delicious snack.' And then before anyone could stop him he gulped it down.

'Very tasty,' he commented, grinning broadly.

The Queen looked rather surprised and moved on quickly to talk to the other guests.

Steinasaurus Rex was behaving perfectly and chatting to everyone, until his tummy started to rumble.

'I'm hungry,' he said in a loud voice.

'Be quiet,' whispered Frank N. Stein. 'Someone will hear you.'

So, without another word Steinasaurus Rex lumbered over to a uniformed man with a chest full of medals and began to munch them.

'He's eating me medals!' shouted the man, 'Get the fella off me!'

But Steinasaurus Rex was not to be stopped. He ate every medal he could find, all the champagne buckets and most of the crockery.

Suddenly a rumour began to go round that someone had taken the diamond broach the Queen was wearing. Frank N. Stein turned white.

'I think it's time we left,' said Mrs Stein firmly and she grabbed the monster by one hand, and they made for home as fast as they could, leaving the other guests to search for the missing broach.

They stopped for a brief moment to have a picture taken of them all dressed up in front of the palace. It turned out to be a very good photograph, except that Steinasaurus Rex grabbed a sword from one of the guards and was eating it just as the snap was taken.

The Queen's broach, needless to say, was never found.

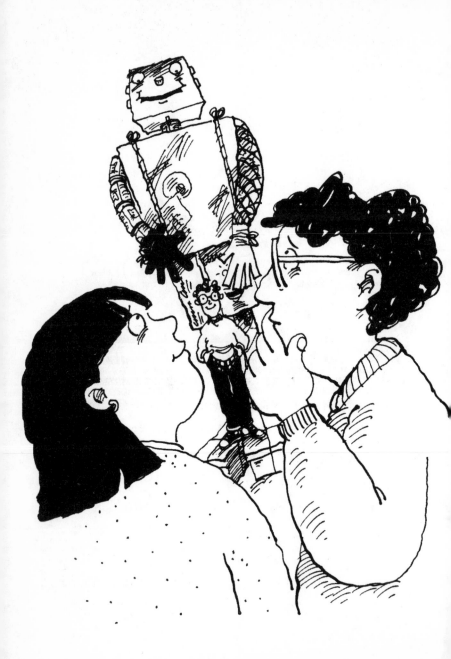

The Monster Hut

'Where we are going to put him I do not know,' said Mr Stein with a sigh, looking at the huge monster his son Frank had made.

'I don't mind where I live,' said the monster cheerfully, 'just so long as I'm not too far from my boy Frank.'

'He can't live in house,' declared Mrs Stein. 'That's for sure.'

'Why not?' demanded the monster, looking tearful. 'Don't you want me?'

Mrs Stein smiled and took the monster's big hand, 'That's not it silly. You can't get in through the doors, remember. You would bang your head on the ceiling. You've eaten so much rubbish you've grown.'

The monster giggled. 'That's right, I'm too big. I could live in the garage. I was made in

a garage, yes the garage would suit me fine.'

'No!' yelled Mr Stein. 'That's where I keep the car. Oh dear, I don't know what I did to deserve this problem.'

It's because you called me Frank Norman Stein,' said his son quickly. 'It's your own fault that you've got to find a home for a monster.'

'I know,' groaned his father. 'We called you Frank after your mother's uncle and Norman after my grandfather. We didn't realise it would lead to you being called Frankenstein.

We didn't think of it at the time.'

'Good thing you didn't,' chortled the monster, 'or I wouldn't be here.'

'I'm glad too,' said Frank gazing affectionately at his monster. 'I never thought I would ever say that I was glad that my name is Frank N. Stein – but I am.'

The monster's eyes filled with tears. He picked Frank up and gave him a big hug.

Just then a team of TV reporters from America turned up and wanted to interview Frank and his monster.

'Could you tell our viewers just how this monster came into being please, Frank?'

Frank took a deep breath and then told his story into the TV camera.

'The kids at school teased me because my name sounded like Frankenstein, so a group of us built this monster out of bits and pieces. Then there was a huge thunder storm and he came alive. Luckily he turned out to be completely harmless – all he wants to do is eat rubbish. Isn't that right, monster?'

The monster beamed and waved. 'It certainly is, my boy Frank. Eat rubbish, that's all I do.' He grabbed the camera. For a terrible moment it looked as though he was about to swallow it whole.

'No!' yelled Frank and his parents and the interviewer together. The monster put the camera down and looked puzzled.

'Is something wrong, Frank?' he asked shaking his big head.

'It's all right, Steinasaurus Rex,' said Frank soothingly. 'You just eat up some of these black sacks of rubbish and leave the camera alone.'

'Is it true that Steinasaurus Rex is called after you, Frank?' asked the interviewer.

'Certainly is,' said the monster, as he munched the final remains of the bag of rubbish. 'After my boy Frank. That's me – Steinasaurus Rex.'

'Is it right that this country no longer has a rubbish disposal problem?'

'Quite right,' said Frank proudly.

'Yes,' agreed the monster, 'I'm never hungry and they don't have any problems with rubbish. It suits everyone.'

When the TV crew had gone, Mrs Stein looked at the monster and sighed.

'We'll have to build a big shed at the bottom of the garden,' she said.

'Where?' demanded her husband.

'Where the vegetable patch is,' said Frank's mother.

'But Mum,' cried Frank. 'You love growing all those lettuces and tomatoes and herbs.'

'Yes I do,' agreed Mrs Stein sadly. 'But the

monster has to have somewhere to live and it has to be near you Frank, so that's the only solution as far as I can see.'

'That's very kind of you, Frank's mum,' said the monster. 'Now show me where you are going to build my house.'

So they walked down to the bottom of the garden, where the rows of lettuces were neatly laid out and the rhubarb and spinach were sprouting.

'Pity about your vegetable patch,' said the monster. 'Those tomatoes look so nice and fresh.'

'Never mind,' said Mrs Stein bravely 'We can manage without.'

The monster looked round and sniffed loudly. 'I'll like it here. There are lots of nice trees and birds singing . . . and what's that lovely smell?'

It's the compost,' said Mrs Stein. 'I'm so sorry, I forgot about that. We'll move it.'

'No need to do that,' cried the monster and ate the lot in two minutes.

'Very nice that was. You can keep on putting compost down there. Then if I get peckish at night I can have a little nibble.'

'Nibble!' shouted Mr Stein. 'You've scoffed the lot. We use it to enrich the soil in the garden. It's not a snack for monsters.'

'Don't worry about that Dad,' said Frank quickly. 'We'll leave some rubbish near the monster's house and I'm sure he'll promise to leave the compost alone. Won't you Steinasaurus Rex?'

'S'pose so, if you say so Frank,' grumbled the monster. 'But that compost is very tasty, very tasty indeed.'

Later that day a van from the Department of the Environment arrived with a wonderful wooden hut for the monster.

'It's very grand,' commented Frank, as the workmen began to put the hut together in the garden.

'Of course,' replied the foreman. 'The Minister said that there was to be nothing but the best for Steinasaurus Rex because he is doing so much good for the country, eating all the rubbish and that.'

The monster grinned and swelled up with pride. 'Nothing but the best for me. Did you hear that Frank?'

'I did,' nodded Frank N. Stein, 'And I agree absolutely. Nothing but the best for my monster.'

By the time the hut was finished it looked wonderful. In front of it were pots full of flowers. Each window had window boxes, and hanging baskets hung over the huge door. Nearby was a dustbin full of rubbish with pots of sweet smelling flowers hanging from it.

'That's for me, if I get peckish in the night,' the monster told the Steins.

'Oh no, all my lovely flowers will be trampled,' said Mrs Stein. 'Oh why didn't we call him Norman Frank and then none of this would have happened!'

'I know dear,' agreed Mr Stein, 'but the monster does make Frank very happy.'

The monster went on living happily at the bottom of the garden. Each day he would eat breakfast with Frank and then go wherever he was needed to eat rubbish.

That is until early one morning. Frank ran down to the hut as he always did, and found the hut empty.

'Monster!' yelled Frank. 'Steinasaurus Rex come here this minute and stop messing around.'

Frank ran around the garden calling out the monsters name. He looked in the neighbouring gardens and out in the street. But there was no sign of the monster anywhere.

Then Frank noticed that the flower pots were smashed and the window boxes broken. Frank felt a sinking feeling in his stomach.

'Steinasaurus Rex is missing! Oh dear, I hope it's just that he got bored and has gone looking for food. I hope he hasn't gone for good.'

Missing

Frank tried not to panic. 'He must have got hungry and gone for a walk that's all,' he thought. 'I hope he only eats rubbish and not anything valuable like a car. I'd better find him before anything awful happens.'

He went in search of his friend. As Frank walked down the street he asked the milkman if he had seen a monster.

The milkman laughed, 'Sorry son, the only monsters I've seen today have had a human form.'

Frank was puzzled, if the monster was anywhere near surely the milkman would have seen him. Then the postman came round the corner.

'My monster's not in his shed,' Frank told the postman. 'Have you seen him?'

'What the great fellow I saw on TV?'

'That's him,' said Frank.

'Oh no, I haven't seen anyone like that. I mean you couldn't miss him, could you?'

'I know,' sighed Frank.

'I'd go and ring the police if I were you,' suggested the postman. 'Someone is sure to have reported him. I bet he's having the time of his life on some rubbish dump.'

'Hope so,' muttered Frank, 'but it's not like him to go wandering off without me.' And he walked home quickly.

As he went back into the house he heard his mum calling.

'Frank is that you?'

'Mum, my monster's disappeared. Have you heard anything?'

'Disappeared!' cried Mrs Stein. 'Don't be silly Frank. How could a huge great thing like that disappear?'

'I don't know mum,' replied Frank, fighting back the tears, 'but he has.'

'I'll call the police,' said Mrs Stein quickly. 'Eat your breakfast while I phone.'

Frank was too worried to eat. He stood beside his mother while she dialled the police station.

'What are they saying?' he asked her. 'Have they seen my monster? Do they know where he is?'

'Be quiet,' hissed his mother. 'I can't hear a word.' And then she said, 'Oh, so there haven't been any reports of sightings. How odd, how very odd. Yes, well please do keep us informed and we'll let you know if we hear anything. I expect there's a simple explanation. Yes, I'll be here all morning so when your people arrive to investigate I can let them in.'

'Where can he be?' demanded Frank, pacing up and down. 'I mean he can't just have disappeared into thin air. Maybe my monster decided he didn't like me after all and ran away.'

'Oh Frank,' said his mum, putting her arms around him. 'Of course that isn't what happened. Now go and get ready for school.'

'You must be joking,' cried Frank. I can't go to school while my monster is lost. I've got to stay here in case he calls and needs me.'

'No, you can't just miss school,' said his

mother. 'But I'll be here all day, and I promise you that if there's any news I'll let you know straight away.'

For the whole morning Frank sat and looked out of the window. He didn't hear one word the teacher said.

At playtime, Jason, Chris, Achmed and Mark crowded around Frank.

'What's up?' they asked.

'I suppose you ought to know what's happened. You did help to build him. Steinasaurus Rex has disappeared.'

'Disappeared!' echoed the boys.

'But that's not possible,' cried Jason. 'He's too big to disappear.'

'I know,' agreed Frank miserably. 'But he has just disappeared.'

The word soon got round that the monster was missing and none of the children did a jot of work that day.

After school, Frank and his friends raced back to Frank's house. The monster had not come back and there had not been any sightings. The police had been round but there were no clues of any kind. Frank was in despair.

That evening, all the children were glued to the television news. Their parent's could hardly persuade them to go to bed. When they arrived at school the next day, each class had a radio on the teachers desk.

'Because this is a special emergency,' the headmaster told the children, 'I have decided to have a news bulletin every half hour, but only on condition that you all do your work as usual.'

The children cheered and every half hour the radio was switched on and you could have heard a pin drop. But there was no news of Steinasaurus Rex.

Interpol had been alerted. All airports, stations and ferry terminals were being watched.

Frank was deluged with letters and cards and telegrams of support from children all over the country. They all promised to look out for the monster and let Frank know if there was any sign of him. But in spite of the search, no one found a single trace of Steinasaurus Rex.

Frank couldn't eat he was so worried. Mr and Mrs Stein worried about Frank and the monster. No one knew what to do next.

Then one morning at breakfast Mrs Stein suddenly grabbed the daily paper and yelled, 'Listen to this! "After many years of silence there are rumblings again in Loch Ness. Nessie, the famous Loch Ness Monster, is said to be haunting the lochs of Scotland. Local residents claim to have seen and heard Nessie for the last eight nights." Ha! This may be the breakthrough we've been waiting for.'

Nessie or Not?

'I don't see what Nessie has got to do with my monster,' muttered Frank, staring gloomily into his glass of orange juice.

'Maybe nothing,' said his father, 'but this is the first mention of a monster since our dear old Steinasaurus Rex disappeared. Who knows – there may be a connection.'

'Yes,' agreed Mrs Stein, 'And next week is half-term.'

'Quite so.' nodded her husband. 'And we've been meaning to take a holiday in Scotland for years.'

'And you're owed a week's holiday,' finished Mrs Stein, 'so I will go into the travel agent this morning and book us a week in Scotland on Loch Ness.'

'But what if my monster wants to get in touch?' demanded Frank. 'He might think that we've abandoned him. I don't think this is a good time to go away.'

'No problem,' said his mother firmly. 'We'll arrange to have the phone manned twenty-four hours a day. So many people want to help, they can take it in turns.'

'Remember the police are watching the house and monitoring all phone calls,' added his father.

'I'd still rather be here,' grumbled Frank.

'Nonsense,' said his father briskly, 'I've got a gut feeling that these sightings of Nessie and the disappearance of our monster are linked.'

A few days later the Steins were on a coach, looking out at the glorious Scottish scenery.

'Look,' cried Mrs Stein, 'Loch Ness.'

'I can't see anything like a monster,' said Frank sadly.

'I know,' agreed his mother. 'And definitely nothing like our monster.

'Give it time, you two,' said Mr Stein, getting their bags down from the rack. 'Give it time.'

Before long the Steins were settled in their hotel room.

'Let's go for a walk and talk to the locals,' said Mum.

'Yes,' agreed Mr Stein enthusiastically. 'Maybe we can glean some information about this mysterious appearance of Nessie, the Loch Ness Monster.'

Frank beamed at his parents.

'I think you really like my monster too,' he said.

'Well yes,' said his mother. 'Even though he has ruined my lovely vegetable patch.'

The Steins walked along the side of the loch. They admired the rolling hills and the smooth outlines of the water, and then went to have tea at the café.

'Did anyone here see the Loch Ness monster?' asked Mr Stein.

'Oh yes,' said the waitress, sitting down with them, ' my cousin's wife's sister's son saw it, clear as the nose on your face.'

'Could we talk to him?' demanded Frank, 'I'm really interested in monsters.'

'You're Frank N. Stein aren't you? I saw you and your wee mother on the television. I'm sorry to hear he's disappeared.'

'We're trying to find him,' Frank told her, 'and any help your cousin's wife's sister's son could give us would be very useful.'

'Do you think he's up here then, your Steinasaurus Rex? Well now, maybe he's courting our Nessie. Is that what you think?'

'We don't know,' said Mr Stein, 'but it does seem a bit of a coincidence that Nessie is active again just when our monster goes missing.'

'True,' said the waitress beginning to get really interested.

'Have any strangers come into the area recently?' asked Frank.

'Och hen, there are always strangers coming here,' replied the waitress. 'This is a tourist area.'

'Hmmm,' said Mrs Stein. 'I think we need to let people know that we are here. Then anyone with any information can get in touch.'

'My husband's mother's brother's third cousin by marriage runs the local paper, should I give him a wee ring?'

'Please,' chorused the Steins.

The next day the headline in the local paper read: "Is Steinasaurus Rex stalking Scotland?" and there was a big picture of Frank and his parents.

'Good,' said Mrs Stein, 'let's see if that

brings in any information.'

Just then the phone rang and they were asked to be on local radio and television.

'This is going just as I planned it,' said Mr Stein smiling. 'Come on, let's go and tell as many people as possible that we are here.'

That evening they had supper at the hotel. During the meal the hotel manager came in to say that there was a phone call for Frank – no one else would do. Frank went and answered the call.

'Frank N. Stein here. Can I help you?'

'No,' came a girl's voice, 'but I can help you. I know where you're monster is.'

'What? Why? Where is he? Are you sure it's him?' asked Frank sharply.

'All he does is call out 'Frank' over and over again. It must be your monster. Please, please won't you come straight away?'

'You bet I will,' said Frank firmly. 'Tell me where to come and I'll be there.'

'I'm in Glen Gordon Castle,' said the girl. 'It's a bit of a way above the loch.'

'Is that the castle I can see from the window?' asked Frank.

'That's the one.'

'But we were told the owner was away and it was empty.'

'That's what they want people to think, but it's not true – there are a lot of people here and they're keeping your monster a prisoner. My name's Morag. You'll know me by my bright red hair. Take care, Frank, these people are dangerous.'

'OK Morag. I'll be there as fast as I can.'

Found?

Frank walked back to his parents with a determined look on his face.

'I think I've tracked him down. I've just had a tip-off from a girl whose mother is the house keeper, up there, at the castle.'

'So what did this girl actually say?' asked Mr Stein.

'She says my monster is being kept prisoner there. She wanted me to go and meet her, and I've promised to go alone.'

'I don't like the sound of that,' interrupted his mother. 'Who knows what kind of people we're dealing with here.'

'I couldn't agree more,' said Mr Stein frowning and looking worried. 'I think we should tell the police immediately.'

'No Dad,' said Frank. 'I promised. I promised that girl . . . and anyway who knows what they might do to my poor monster if the police turned up. No, I have to go alone.'

'I'm not happy about it,' said Mrs Stein.

'Me neither,' agreed her husband, putting his arm around her.

'Well you know where I'm going,' said Frank pointing up the hill.

'And if you're not back in one hour we'll send the police in, promise or no promise,' said Mr Stein firmly.

'Fair enough,' said Frank. He raced out of the hotel and ran even faster up the hill and out of sight.

As he was running along Frank heard a car and looked up. It was a taxi. He flagged it down and jumped in.

'To the castle,' he panted, 'as fast as you can!'

'Are you the laddie that lost his monster?' asked the cab driver.

'Yes,' said Frank. 'Do you know anything about him.'

'Well, I'm not sure if I do or not. I was driving some people home the other night and I saw a huge creature wandering over the mountains, banging his chest and yelling something like, "Thanks, thanks!" My wife says I must have been drinking.'

'Did you tell the police?' asked Frank.

'I did not. People are always reporting monsters here, the police get sick of it.'

'So if you wanted to imprison a monster, Loch Ness would be a good place to do it?'

'Aye, that could be right. but who would want to imprison a monster, young man?'

'I don't know, but that is precisely what

I'm hoping to find out,' Frank told him. 'Stop! Stop here please, I need to get out.'

'I can't leave you here, laddie, all on your own on a deserted road. Let me take you right up to the castle.'

'No, no thank you. This is fine.'

'I'll just wait here a wee moment and see that you're all right.'

'No, no please don't. I need to be alone.'

'Well OK, if that's what you want. But I'm not too happy about it.'

Frank watched as the cab drove away down the hill. It was getting dark, he began to feel nervous.

Suddenly he heard the crunch of footsteps on gravel. Frank's heart raced as he ran and hid behind a rock.

'It's all right Frank,' came a voice. 'It's only me – Morag.' A girl with bright red curls jumped down next to him.

'Hello,' said Frank, holding his hand out formally.

'Hi,' said Morag.

'Can you tell me what's going on?' asked Frank.

'Not really because I don't understand myself,' she replied.

'They've got your monster locked up in the castle. He was in chains at first.'

'And he ate them?' said Frank smiling.

'I think so,' agreed the girl smiling back.

'But why do they want my monster?'

'I told you, I don't know. I think they want him to eat something.'

'My monster eats anything,' Frank told her. 'Why would anyone want to kidnap him just for that?'

'I don't understand it neither does your monster.'

'Have you talked to him?'

'Yes, I was so sorry for him. But all he could tell me was that they wanted him to eat something but he's not hungry because he misses you. So all he does is cry and say he wants his boy Frank. That's why I helped him escape.'

'Escape!'

'Yes, I unlocked the door of the cell while those horrible men were watching television. He ran away but they caught up with him pretty quickly.'

'My poor monster,' cried Frank. 'Why didn't you tell anyone about him?'

'My mum said I was to keep quiet, she's worried about her job. After I stole the key of the monsters cell, she thought she would get into trouble. She's been unemployed for years you see. But I phoned the paper with that story about the Loch Ness Monster I thought it would give you a clue.'

'It was a great idea,' said Frank, 'and it certainly worked. Mum and Dad insisted we get here straightaway.'

'I know, and I was going to leave it to you after that, but the monster is so miserable. He won't eat a thing and I couldn't bear it any more . . . so in the end I rang you up.'

'You're great, Morag. Steinasaurus Rex and I will never be able to repay you.'

'We'll worry about that after we rescue him. Come on! Let's go and see exactly what's going on in the castle.'

To The Rescue!

Frank and Morag climbed up the slopes to the castle. Morag quietly opened the back door and Frank followed her upstairs. As they got nearer the heart of the castle they heard great sighs and sobs.

'Frank, I want my boy Frank!' a voice moaned.

'My poor monster,' thought Frank, trying hard not to cry.

Then he heard, 'Take it away. I don't want to eat anything – not until you bring my boy here.'

'I wish we could get our hands on that Frank N. Stein,' came a man's angry voice. 'Maybe he would get this stupid monster to eat and then we could all get out of here.'

'I don't like being here anymore than you

do but we agreed to get rid of this nuclear waste and get rid of it we will,' said another man's voice.

'Yeah, he's got to eat it. I mean we're sitting on a gold mine. We could get nuclear waste from all over the world.'

'I know . . . just think, no one knows what to do with the stuff – they'd pay us any money to get it off their hands. We'll be rich. Sooner or later this brute will get hungry and do our work for us, don't you worry.'

Frank had frozen with horror.

'Nuclear waste, they want my poor monster to eat nuclear waste!' he cried.

'Come on Steinasaurus,' said one of the men. 'Eat this up and you can go free, you can go back to your boy.'

'Yeah,' said the other voice. 'You must be getting very hungry. It's days since you ate. Come on – have a nice little snack now and then maybe a proper big supper later.'

'Do you promise that I can see my boy if I eat this?'

'We do.'

'Cross your hearts and hope to die?'

'Cross our hearts and hope to die.'

'Oh all right then, give it here. You're right I am a bit peckish.'

At that moment Frank burst in through the door, 'No! Don't Steinasaurus Rex! Don't even take a little bite.'

'Frank, my boy Frank!' cried the monster, breaking into a huge smile.

'Put me down Steinasaurus,' yelled Frank. 'This is very serious.'

'I'm pleased to see you, my boy Frank. I'll just eat what these men want me to eat and then we can go home.'

'No!' screamed Frank 'Don't touch it.'

'Come on, Frank, I'm hungry. I missed my boy so much I didn't eat a thing. But now you're here I feel like my old self again and I'm starving.'

The monster picked up one of the metal canisters with a skull and cross bones on it'

'Look!' yelled Frank, 'That sign means what's inside is poisonous.'

'Not to a monster,' said one of the men.

'That's right,' agreed the monster, lifting the canister to his mouth.

'No, put it down!' yelled Frank at the top of his voice. 'If you eat that you will never be able to live near me or any other person. Put it down, please put it down!'

The monster dropped the canister on the floor. It fell with a thud on the foot of one of the kidnappers. He jumped up and down in pain.

'Now why would that be Frank? Why wouldn't you want to be my friend if I ate this stuff?'

'Because it's radio-active monster. People get very ill if they come into contact with radio-active material. Everyone would run away from you.'

'Even you, my boy Frank?'

'Yes, even me.'

The monster glared at his kidnappers. 'You wanted me to eat something that would mean I could never be near my boy Frank. That makes me very cross.'

The monster thumped his chest angrily and ran towards the two men. They went white with terror and raced to the door.

The monster followed them shouting and shrieking.

'I'll get you for trying to make me eat that stuff. Just you wait!'

'No, Steinasaurus, come back,' called Frank.

But the monster took no notice. he chased the men down the stairs and through the kitchens out into the castle grounds, shouting 'Wait till I get you! I'll munch and crunch you, oh yes I will!'

The two men ran over the drawbridge but when they saw the police coming towards them, they turned and ran back again. They were trapped between the monster, and the police and Mr and Mrs Stein. They decided there was only one thing to do. They jumped off the drawbridge and into the moat. The monster jumped in after them and they scrambled up the other bank into the arms of the police.

'Save us,' they shouted 'We surrender, the monster is after us. We confess, we admit everything. We did it all, we'll answer all your questions, just save us from Steinasaurus Rex!'

'Get them into the van quickly,' said the Police Chief, as the monster charged towards them yelling.

'I'll get you . . . trying to separate me from my boy. You just wait till I catch up with you. There'll be some crunching done!'

The two men cowered in the back of the police van.

'Drive on!' instructed the Police Chief. 'Get them out of here.'

'Where's Frank?' demanded Mrs Stein. 'Is he all right, where's my son?'

'I'm here mum, I'm fine,' called Frank, as he ran panting out of the building, followed by Morag. 'This is my friend Morag, she helped me find my monster. Her mum works in the castle and Morag heard Steinasaurus crying. It was Morag who got the rumours going about Nessie.'

'Congratulations Morag, and thank you very much,' cried mr Stein.

Mrs Stein gave the monster a big hug. 'Glad to see you Steinasaurus Rex, we've all been so worried.'

'What was going on in the castle?' asked the Police Chief.

'Those men kidnapped my monster. They planned to make their fortunes by getting my monster to eat all of the nuclear waste that people don't know what to do with.'

'Nuclear waste! That is serious, is it in the castle?'

'Yes,' said Frank 'And my monster nearly ate it because he didn't understand.'

'Call in some back-up,' snapped the Police Chief into his radio. 'There's nuclear waste in that castle. No-one is to be allowed in. Get the government to take it away. No one else is to touch it.'

He turned to the Steins, 'Those kidnappers will be up on a serious charge,' he told them. 'Illegally disposing of nuclear waste, why that could kill thousands of people. Trying to get your monster to eat it indeed.'

'Talking about eating,' said the monster,

'I'm hungry. I haven't eaten for over a week.'

And he went over to a police car and ate it in two gulps.

'That's better,' he said grinning at the horrified group. 'Now I'm back with my boy Frank and I'm not hungry anymore, what more could a monster want?'

The Steins looked at each other in horror.

'Sorry about the car,' mumbled Mr Stein, 'he only does that when he's very hungry indeed.'

'I should hope so! I've never seen anything like it in my life,' said the Police Chief. 'Still it's a small price to pay to catch villains who are messing around with nuclear waste. Well done, Frank, for helping to catch them. Now excuse me a minute while I sort out a wee problem.'

The police chief picked up his radio again and said, 'Send a large lorry round here quickly, and I mean yesterday. Destination the municipal rubbish dump!'